Ludacris

by C.F. Earl

Superstars of Hip-Hop

Ludacris

by C.F. Earl

Mason Crest

Ludacris

Mason Crest
370 Reed Road
Broomall, Pennsylvania 19008
www.masoncrest.com

Printed and bound in the United States of America.

First printing
9 8 7 6 5 4 3 2 1

Library of Congress Cataloging-in-Publication Data

Earl, C. F.
  Ludacris / by C.F. Earl.
     p. cm. – (Superstars of hip hop)
  Includes index.
  ISBN 978-1-4222-2523-3 (hard cover) – ISBN 978-1-4222-2508-0 (series hardcover) – ISBN 978-1-4222-9225-9 (ebook)
 1. Ludacris (Rapper)–Juvenile literature. 2. Rap musicians–United States–Biography–Juvenile literature. I. Title.
  ML3930.L85E27 2012
  782.421649092–dc23
  [B]
                        2011019649

Produced by Harding House Publishing Service, Inc.
www.hardinghousepages.com
Interior Design by MK Bassett-Harvey.
Cover design by Torque Advertising & Design.

Publisher's notes:
  • All quotations in this book come from original sources and contain the spelling and grammatical inconsistencies of the original text.
  • The Web sites mentioned in this book were active at the time of publication. The publisher is not responsible for Web sites that have changed their addresses or discontinued operation since the date of publication. The publisher will review and update the Web site addresses each time the book is reprinted.

DISCLAIMER: The following story has been thoroughly researched, and to the best of our knowledge, represents a true story. While every possible effort has been made to ensure accuracy, the publisher will not assume liability for damages caused by inaccuracies in the data, and makes no warranty on the accuracy of the information contained herein. This story has not been authorized nor endorsed by Ludacris.

Contents

Hip-Hop lingo

Each year, the National Academy of Recording Arts and Sciences gives out the Grammy Awards (short for Gramophone Awards)—or **Grammys**—to people who have done something really big in the music industry.

Charity is doing something to help make people's lives better.

A **rapper** is someone who chants rhymes, often off the top of his head, sometimes with music in the background.

If a person has **challenged** someone, he has dared him to try to beat him in a contest.

Open-mic is a kind of show where the audience can take part by performing into the microphone.

Responsibility is a sense of duty to follow through with a task.

An **intern** is a person who works at a job to learn about the work, instead of to make money.

DJ is short for disc jockey. A DJ plays music on the radio or at a party and announces the songs.

An **album** has a bunch of songs made to go together.

A **recording** is a sound or video that has been saved on a computer or a CD.

Chapter 1

Chris Before Luda

Ludacris was taking home three **Grammys** at the 2007 Awards. He won Best Rap Album and Best Rap Song. That night Ludacris performed with Mary J. Blige. Together, the two performed "Runaway Love."

The 2007 Awards show was proof that Ludacris could do anything. He was acting in movies. He was helping kids through his work with **charity**. And he'd become a very successful **rapper**. Now he was taking home Grammy Awards.

Ludacris may be a star today, but he had to work hard to get there. The Grammy Awards were a long way from where he grew up.

An MC Is Born

Ludacris was born on September 11, 1977. His real name is Christopher Bridges. Chris was born in Champaign, Illinois.

His mom, Roberta, and his dad, Wayne, were young when Chris was born. They were still in college.

Soon, Chris's parents broke up. He and his mom lived together in Illinois. Things were tough for Chris and Roberta sometimes. But

Roberta gave Chris love and support. She worked hard to make his life better.

Growing up, Chris always loved rap and hip-hop. At nine, he wrote his first verses. No matter what life was like at home, Chris had rap. Music was something he could use to get away from things that were bothering him.

Chris loved to rap for his friends and family. He rhymed during lunch. He rapped for his middle school classmates.

When Chris was twelve, he joined his first hip-hop group. They were called the Loudmouth Hooligans.

Chris was already moving toward success as a rapper. He loved music and wanted to make his own.

But soon after joining the Loudmouth Hooligans, Chris left Illinois. Chris and his mom moved to Atlanta, Georgia. Chris started going to Banneker High School.

At his new school, Chris kept on rapping. He spit out verses in the lunchroom. He even **challenged** his classmates to rap battles. Soon, people knew Chris Bridges had skills.

Taking on other students was good practice for Chris. Soon, he'd be going to talent shows and **open-mic** nights. Chris was on his way to being a rap star.

Life in Atlanta

Chris's time in Atlanta was mostly happy. But he and his mom also had a lot to overcome. They didn't have much money, so life could be difficult. At one time, Chris and his mom lived in one room in someone else's house.

Roberta always told Chris that school was very important. She knew that education was the best way to succeed. She also taught Chris about saving money. She taught him about **responsibility**.

Roberta wanted Chris to be the best he could be. She wanted him to be able to take care of himself, too.

Chris kept rapping and going to school. He loved music more and more. But his schoolwork was important to him, too. He wanted to make his mom proud.

While earning his degree in music management, Chris worked for station Hot 97.5 in Atlanta. It wasn't long before rap fans found Chris, and the station made him a DJ. His fame and popularity continued to grow, and Chris Lova Lova became a local celebrity.

When Chris was finishing high school, he had a choice to make. Would he go to college or try to make it in music? Lots of rappers don't go to college. But Chris knew how important learning was. He knew that it wasn't easy to become a rapper. He'd need something to fall back on.

Chris decided to go to Georgia State University. He wanted to be a rapper, but he also understood business. So he chose to take music management. It mixed his love for rap and his skills in school. Now he could learn about the business of music.

Chris Lova Lova

In college, Chris became an **intern** at Atlanta radio station Hot 97.5. He tried to learn as much as he could there. He also started to make a name for himself at the job.

Chris showed the people he worked with that he could rap. When they saw his skill, they let him rap on some ads for the station. Soon, Chris was a **DJ** at the station.

Chris's DJ name was Chris Lova Lova. People liked Chris's voice and his personality. He became one of the most popular DJs at Hot 97.5.

Sometimes Chris would rap over the hit songs he played on the radio. Lots of people listened just to hear Chris rap. Chris Lova Lova's raps became famous in the area.

Soon, Chris was chosen to have a nighttime show for Hot 97.5. All the while, Chris was saving his money. He hadn't given up on his own dreams. He still wanted to go out on his own as a rapper.

On the radio, Chris finally had lots of people who listened to him rap. He even had fans. It was a small taste of the life Chris would have later on.

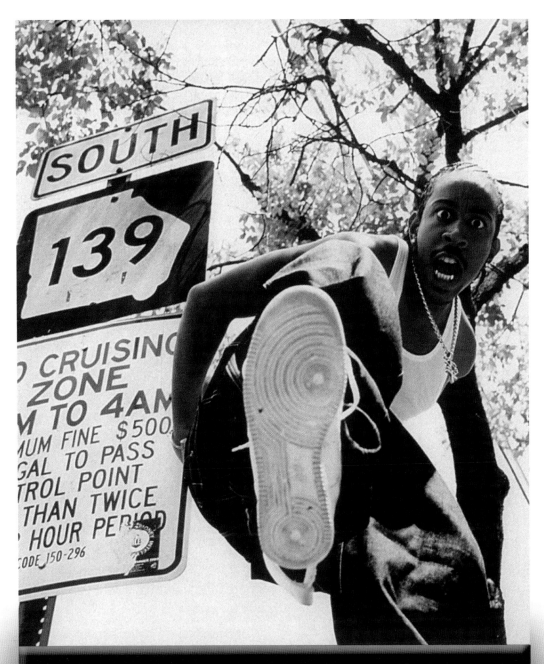

Chris Bridges' hip-hop star needed his own identity, and he decided on Ludacris. The name reflects the two sides of Chris's personality, calm and collected but crazy; and describes his music's ludicrous lyrics and performances. Whatever the reasons behind it, the name is unforgettable.

Ludacris Is Born

Chris was Chris Lova Lova for three years. Chris wanted to make music more than anything, though. He thought he was ready to make his own **album**. He wanted to take his shot at making it in rap.

First, Chris wanted to change his name. Chris Lova Lova was a great name for a radio DJ. But Chris needed another name for his rap career. Chris needed an MC name that would let people know who he was.

Chris called himself Ludacris. It was a name that matched Chris's style and personality. Chris says he can be calm and quiet. He can also be funny and full of energy. Sometimes he's even a little crazy.

The name Ludacris matched Chris's lyrics and shows, too. His lyrics could be over-the-top and wild. His shows were fun and exciting. Ludacris was the perfect name for Chris.

With his new name, Ludacris was ready to make his first album. He had saved money by working at Hot 95.7. Now he had enough to make his dreams come true.

Ludacris knew about the business of music. He had learned about it at college and at Hot 95.7. He knew it could be hard to make and sell an album by yourself. Most albums are made with help from record companies.

Ludacris didn't have that kind of help. But it didn't matter to him. He was going to make an album anyway.

In 1999, Ludacris recorded his first album. It was called *Incognegro*. Ludacris paid for the **recording** himself. He sold the album out of the trunk of his car. A copy cost seven dollars. He tried to get lots of people to hear his music. He sold his album after shows and wherever he could.

Ludacris sold 50,000 copies of his album. It wasn't long before the music business paid attention. Ludacris was a local star in Atlanta. Soon, he'd be known all over the country and the world.

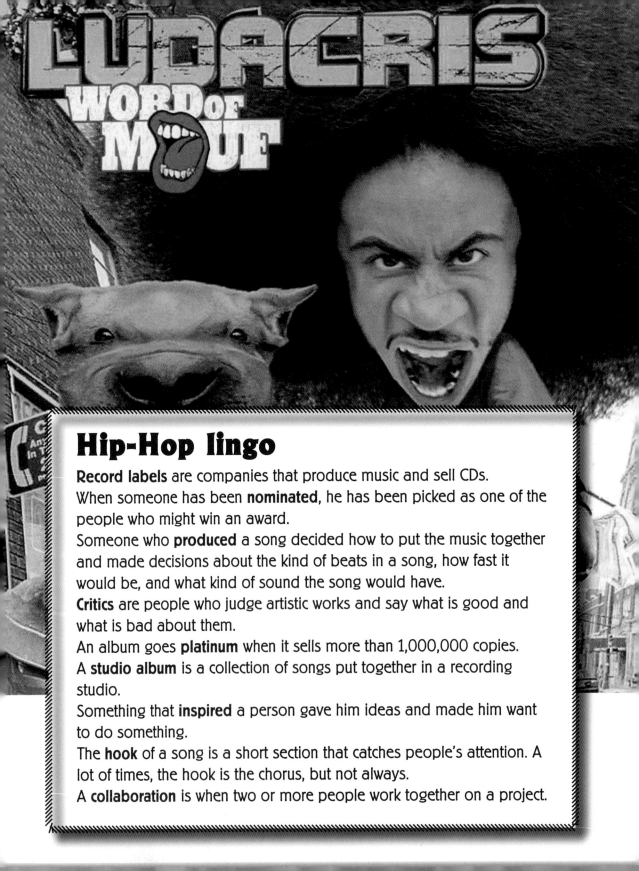

Hip-Hop lingo

Record labels are companies that produce music and sell CDs.

When someone has been **nominated**, he has been picked as one of the people who might win an award.

Someone who **produced** a song decided how to put the music together and made decisions about the kind of beats in a song, how fast it would be, and what kind of sound the song would have.

Critics are people who judge artistic works and say what is good and what is bad about them.

An album goes **platinum** when it sells more than 1,000,000 copies.

A **studio album** is a collection of songs put together in a recording studio.

Something that **inspired** a person gave him ideas and made him want to do something.

The **hook** of a song is a short section that catches people's attention. A lot of times, the hook is the chorus, but not always.

A **collaboration** is when two or more people work together on a project.

Chapter 2

Making It Big as Ludacris

Ludacris's first album was a huge success for someone starting out. He didn't have a big company behind him. He'd done all the work on his own. Most people thought you couldn't succeed in music without help. Ludacris had proven them wrong.

Ludacris signed with Def Jam Records in 2000. He had been selling CDs from his car. Now he was part of one of the biggest rap **record labels** in the world. Ludacris was on his way to being a star.

Def Jam put out *Incognegro* again under the name *Back for the First Time*. The album was sold for the first time in October 2000. Very quickly, it became a hit. The album sold more than three million copies!

Songs like "Southern Hospitality" and "What's Your Fantasy?" helped Ludacris become even more popular. He joined with Timbaland to record a song called "Phat Rabbit." His songs could be heard in clubs, on TV, or on the radio. The new rapper seemed to be everywhere.

Def Jam saw that Southern rap was becoming more popular. The Southern rap sound had more fans than ever. Ludacris was a big part of why Southern rap became better known. Def Jam decided to make a new label for Ludacris and other Southern rappers. They called it Def Jam South.

Ludacris was one of the biggest stars on Def Jam South. His music had helped bring the Southern rap sound to more people than ever. Chris Bridges was finally the rapper he'd always wanted to be. And he was just getting started.

Word of Mouf

On November 27, 2001, Ludacris released his second album. This one was called *Word of Mouf.*

Word of Mouf sold almost 300,000 copies in its first week. Over the next eight years, the album sold more than three and a half million copies. It is Ludacris's best-selling album.

Ludacris's song "Rollout" was the first hit from *Word of Mouf.* Timbaland **produced** the song. He had helped Ludacris on his first album, too.

"Rollout" was **nominated** for a MTV Video Music Award in 2002. For the awards show, Ludacris performed "Rollout" on top of a moving bus. Fans lined the sides of the New York City streets to see him.

"Rollout" wasn't the only hit from *Word of Mouf.* Songs like "Saturday (Oooh Oooh)" and "Area Codes" did very well, too. They are still some of Ludacris's most well-known songs.

In 2002, Ludacris was up for three Grammys. He was nominated for the song "Area Codes." He was also nominated for the music video for "One Minute Man." And he was nominated for his album *Back for the First Time.*

The next year, *Word of Mouf* was nominated for Best Rap Album at the Grammys. "Rollout" was also nominated, for Best Male Rap Solo Performance.

Word of Mouf was a huge success. Ludacris was becoming one of the greatest rappers in the world.

Ludacris and Bill O'Reilly

With new fans came new **critics**. Though many people loved Ludacris's music, some saw it as a problem.

In 2002, Ludacris let Pepsi use one of his songs in an ad. Having the song play on TV was great for Ludacris. It meant more people would get to hear his music. Ludacris's music helped Pepsi speak to young people. Not everyone liked Pepsi using Ludacris's music, though.

In August, Fox News TV host Bill O'Reilly slammed Ludacris. He told his audience that Ludacris's songs were bad for kids. O'Reilly said that Ludacris's song was hurting America's young people.

Along with new, more mainstream fans came new critics, especially from the more conservative element of society. Pepsi quickly dropped Ludacris's music from one of its commercials when Fox television talk-show host Bill O'Reilly complained about the lyrics.

O'Reilly even told his fans to stop buying Pepsi because of the ad. Soon, Pepsi took Ludacris's song out of the commercial.

Pepsi chose to use Ozzy Osbourne's family in the ad instead of Ludacris. This made many supporters of Ludacris mad. They said that Pepsi had chosen people who used just as many bad words as Ludacris.

Some said that it was only because Ludacris was black that he was taken out of the ad. The Osbournes had not been good role models, people said, but no one complained when Pepsi chose them for the ad.

Others said that Ludacris's music was why he was taken out of the ad. They said it had nothing to do with his race.

Ludacris was angry with Bill O'Reilly. He was also angry with Pepsi. He didn't let it slow him down, though. Soon, he was back with a new album. He also had strong words for critics like O'Reilly.

Chicken N Beer

In the spring of 2003, before his next album, Ludacris put out two new songs. "Act a Fool" was from the soundtrack to the movie *2 Fast 2 Furious*. Ludacris had acted in the movie, too. The second song was called "P-Poppin'." Neither song was a hit, but Ludacris was ready to release his next album.

Chicken N Beer came out in the fall of 2003. This new album was the best-selling album in the country in its first week.

On *Chicken N Beer*, Ludacris fought back against his critics. In a verse on the song "Blow it Out," Ludacris even uses Bill O'Reilly's name. Through his music, he got back at the talk-show host.

The video for "Blow It Out" was different than Ludacris's others. Fans were used to seeing colorful, funny videos from Ludacris. "Blow It Out" had a dark look to it. In the video, Ludacris raps into the camera while standing on the street.

HE'S THE MAN WITH THE DIRTIEST MOUTH IN THE GAME, BUT
DON'TCHA LOVE HIM FOR IT? BOW DOWN TO THE KING OF COMEDY

MUCH MORE MOUF

Feature Zone: Ludacris 'Mouf: Haile Columnist

If critics such as Bill O'Reilly thought they could put an end to Ludacris's career, or at least make the artist change how he did things, they could not have been more wrong. He refused to compromise his beliefs to please others.

The video ends with an explosion. The message was clear. Mess with Ludacris, and he'll take you down in his music.

Chicken N Beer's biggest hit was called "Stand Up." Kanye West had produced it, and it quickly hit number one. It was also featured on the soundtrack to the movie *Honey*.

The album was Ludacris's third to go **platinum**. *Chicken N Beer* sold more than two million copies.

The following February, at the 2004 Grammys, Ludacris was nominated for three awards. One song, "Act a Fool," was up for the Best Song Written for a Motion Picture or Television Special. Another, "Gossip Folks," was nominated for Best Rap Performance.

Red Light District

Just one year after *Chicken N Beer* came out, Ludacris was back again. He called his fourth **studio album** *The Red Light District*.

The Red Light District came out on December 7, 2004. In it's first week, it sold more than 300,000 copies. That made it the number-one album in the country that week.

The first single from the album was called "Get Back." The video for the song had Ludacris dressed up as the Hulk. As the Hulk, Ludacris used his giant fists to smash through walls.

The next single from *The Red Light District* was called "Number One Spot." The song was **inspired** by the Austin Powers movies and used samples of the Austin Powers theme music.

On another song from the album, "Pimpin' All Over the World," Bobby Valentino sang the **hook**. The song was popular, and it helped launch Bobby Valentino—or Bobby V, as he is now better known—as an artist.

In January 2005, Ludacris was the musical guest on *Saturday Night Live*. With the band Sum 41, he played a rock version of his song "Get Back." This helped even more people get to know him and his music.

In 2005, Ludacris won his first Grammy Award. He had rapped on Usher's song "Yeah." The song had been a huge hit. In fact, it was one of the most popular songs of 2005. It won the Grammy for Best Rap/Sung **Collaboration**.

Ludacris was on top of the world. He'd become one of rap's biggest names. His albums were selling millions. Ludacris was still going strong, too. He still had plenty of talent to show the world.

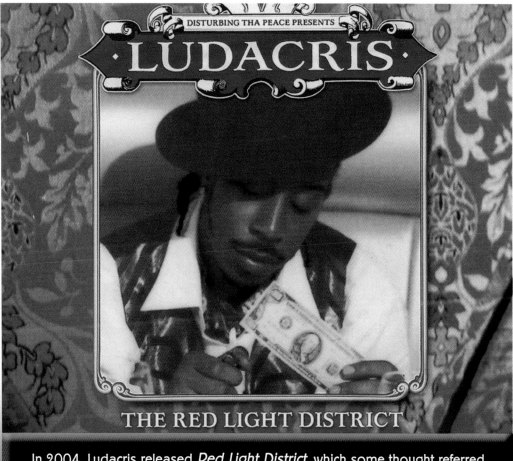

In 2004, Ludacris released *Red Light District,* which some thought referred to a section in Amsterdam where drugs and prostitution are legal. Not so, says Ludacris. According to him, the title refers to a state of mind with no limitations.

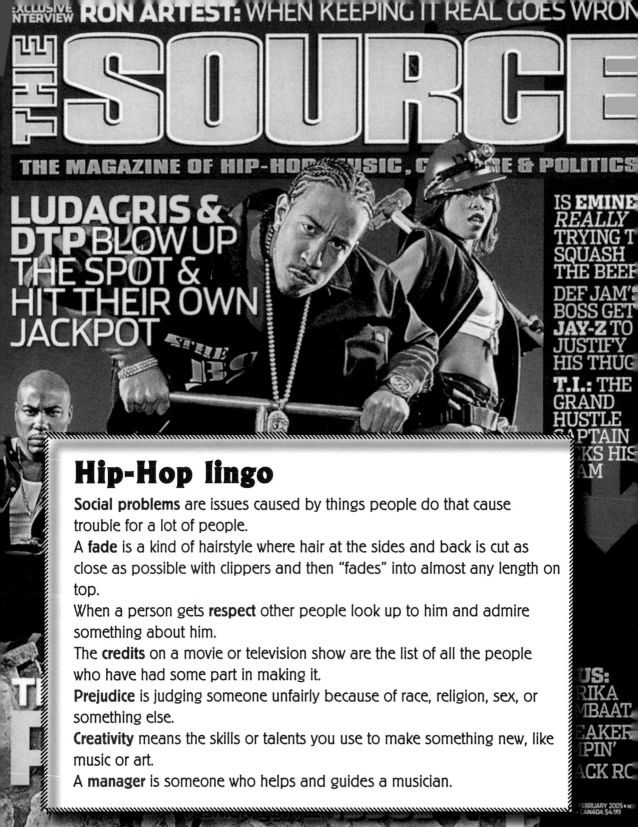

THE SOURCE

THE MAGAZINE OF HIP-HOP MUSIC, CULTURE & POLITICS

**LUDACRIS &
DTP** BLOW UP
THE SPOT &
HIT THEIR OWN
JACKPOT

IS **EMINE**
REALLY
TRYING T
SQUASH
THE BEEF

DEF JAM'
BOSS GET
JAY-Z TO
JUSTIFY
HIS THUG

T.I.: THE
GRAND
HUSTLE
CAPTAIN
KS HIS
AM

Hip-Hop lingo

Social problems are issues caused by things people do that cause trouble for a lot of people.

A **fade** is a kind of hairstyle where hair at the sides and back is cut as close as possible with clippers and then "fades" into almost any length on top.

When a person gets **respect** other people look up to him and admire something about him.

The **credits** on a movie or television show are the list of all the people who have had some part in making it.

Prejudice is judging someone unfairly because of race, religion, sex, or something else.

Creativity means the skills or talents you use to make something new, like music or art.

A **manager** is someone who helps and guides a musician.

US:
RIKA
MBAAT.

EAKER
PIN'

ACK RC

FEBRUARY 2005 • N
CANADA $4.99

WWW.THESOURCE.COM

Chapter 3

Seizing the Day

Ludacris was still focused on making the best music he could. He wanted to get better and better. On his next album, Ludacris was ready to do just that.

Ludacris's fifth album was called *Release Therapy*. The album came out on September 26, 2006. In its first week, it hit number one. That made it Ludacris's third number-one album in a row.

Release Therapy was different than Ludacris's other albums. Ludacris told his fans this album would be more serious. The first part of the album would be *Release*. This part would have songs about Ludacris getting things off his chest. Most of these songs would be serious.

The second part was *Therapy*. This part would have songs about feeling good. *Therapy* was about trying to deal with problems by having fun.

The first single from *Release Therapy* was called "Money Maker." Pharell produced the song and rapped on it. "Money Maker" quickly became a number-one hit. His next single from the album, "Grew Up a Screw Up," featured Young Jeezy. The third single, "Runaway

Love," is a serious song. Mary J. Blige sings the hook. Ludacris tells the stories of young girls growing up through hard times.

Ludacris was starting to use his music to talk about **social problems**. Many of his fans liked that. Ludacris was making music about what life is really like for people.

The cover of *Release Therapy* shows Ludacris with a new haircut. He'd always been known for his cornrows. Now, he wore his hair in a short **fade**. He was showing the world things were different now. His music had changed. He'd changed. Chris Bridges had grown up. But Ludacris had a lot more to give.

At the 2007 Grammy Awards, Ludacris won two Grammys. *Release Therapy* won Best Rap Album. "Money Maker" won Best Rap Song. These were the first Grammys Ludacris had won for his own work.

Ludacris' music was now getting **respect** and awards. *Release Therapy* had taken Ludacris to places other rappers dreamed of.

From Atlanta to the Academy Awards

With Ludacris's success came chances to try new things. Ludacris wanted to try acting, but he was worried. He wanted to be taken seriously. He didn't want to look like a rapper trying to act. He wanted to be a real actor.

To help separate the actor from the rapper, Ludacris used his full name when acting. In **credits** he was listed as Chris "Ludacris" Bridges.

Ludacris' first big role was in the movie *2 Fast 2 Furious*. He played Tej, a former street racer. The movie did well in theaters. Until then, most people had only known about Ludacris from his music. For fans, this was a chance to see Ludacris doing something new. For everyone, it was a chance to see Ludacris show another side of himself.

Ludacris got an even bigger chance to act in 2005. He played Anthony in the movie *Crash*. The movie was about how people view each other. It also talked about race and **prejudice**. Don Cheadle, Terrance Howard, Matt Dillon, and Sandra Bullock—big-name actors—starred in the movie with Ludacris.

In the Oscar-winning film *Crash*, Ludacris plays Anthony (shown here with Larenz Tate, who played Peter), who doesn't like the influence hip-hop has on African Americans. Because he wants to be taken seriously as an actor, he often uses the name Chris "Ludacris" Bridges.

The 2005 film *Crash* was a huge success and the actors formed a special bond. Here, Chris, Matt Dillon, Don Cheadle, and Terrence Howard show off their awards as winners of the Screen Actors Guild Award for Outstanding Performance by a Cast in a Motion Picture.

Crash was different from *2 Fast 2 Furious*. *Crash* was a serious adult movie. Ludacris worked hard to make sure he was doing his best. During filming, he asked for help from the other actors.

The movie was a huge success. People enjoyed the story. It also made them think about problems like prejudice. In 2006, *Crash* won the Oscar for Best Picture at the Academy Awards. That's the highest award a movie can get.

That same year, Ludacris and the other actors in *Crash* won another award. They all won the Screen Actors Guild Award for Outstanding Performance by an Ensemble Cast. People could see how well they had worked together. The Screen Actors Guild was saying they were all great actors, including Ludacris.

Chris costars with Terrence Howard in *Hustle and Flow* as a hometown rapper who found success in the hip-hop world. Howard plays a rap "wannabe," who wants Chris's character to listen to his demo tape. Though Chris's screen time is short it's an important role.

Two months after *Crash* was released, Ludacris appeared in another movie, *Hustle & Flow*. This movie was about a rapper trying to make it. Terrance Howard, who had also been in Crash, plays the rapper, named DJay. Ludacris plays Skinny Black. Black is a rapper who has been changed by fame and success. Ludacris knew all about how hard it was not to let success change you.

Over the next few years, Ludacris kept acting. He was in two episodes of *Law and Order: Special Victims Unit*. Then he played Mickey in *RocknRolla*, a movie about a crime boss in London. His next movie, *Max Payne*, was based on a video game with the same name. In *Max Payne*, Ludacris played a good cop named Jim Bravura. In 2009, Ludacris was in a movie called *Gamer*.

Ludacris used to be known just for his music. Today, people know that Chris "Ludacris" Bridges is more than a rapper. His acting has helped people to see him differently. Now they understand Ludacris's music is just one way he shows his **creativity**.

Ludacris the Businessman

When Ludacris was first trying to make it in music, he had started Disturbing tha Peace (DTP). DTP was a record label. Together with his **manager**, Chaka Zulu, Ludacris had put out his first album.

DTP had also helped put out Ludacris's other albums. By working with Def Jam and Universal Music Group, DTP has put out many albums. Ludacris's friend Bobby Valentino put his first two albums out on DTP in 2005. Rapper Chingy has also worked with Disturbing tha Peace. In 2008, rapper Lil Scrappy signed up with DTP.

Disturbing tha Peace has been part of Ludacris's life since he started in music. DTP has been there for him. And he's been there for DTP. Today, Ludacris and Chaka Zulu run DTP together.

Ludacris has put his music management degree to work as well. As CEO of Disturbing tha Peace Records, he is giving young artists such as Bobby Valentino (seen here with Ludacris at the 2004 Prism Awards) a helping hand in the music world.

In a return to his radio roots, in 2005, Ludacris announced that he would host an XM Satellite Radio show. When he appeared at NASDAQ with XM CEO Hugh Panero, Ludacris became the first hip-hop artist to ring the stock exchange's opening bell.

DTP gives Ludacris the chance to use his education in music management. He uses what he learned at Hot 98.7, too. Ludacris has always been a businessman. Selling his own music was just one way he showed it.

Disturbing tha Peace hasn't been Ludacris's only business, though. Ludacris has also worked with XM Satellite Radio. He hosted a radio show called *Disturbing tha Peace Presents: Ludacris's Open Mic*. He was perfect for the work, thanks to his time at Hot 98.7. At XM Radio, Ludacris could show the world the music he liked.

Through his work at XM Radio, Ludacris became the first rapper to ever open the New York Stock Exchange. On September 29, 2005, he and the head of XM Radio rang the opening bell.

Ludacris has also worked with TAG Body Spray. As part of their line of celebrity "Signature Series," he created his own scent of body spray called "Get Yours." People could vote for which celebrity scent they liked best. Whoever got the most votes would win money for a charity. Ludacris was supporting the Ludacris Foundation.

Ludacris was a successful rapper, actor, and businessman. He'd done more in a few years than many artists did in their whole lives. But he wanted to do more. He'd tried acting. He'd given business a shot. Now, he was ready to get back to the music.

Hip-Hop lingo

The **singles chart** is a list of the best-selling songs for a week.
A **remix** is a new version of a song that has already been on an earlier CD.

Chapter 4

Ludacris's Show Goes On

Ludacris had done a lot of great things in just a few years. He'd acted in movies and on TV. He'd made big business deals. He'd helped other artists break into the business. But music had always been most important to him.

Ludacris next album, *Theater of the Mind*, came out on November 22, 2008. *Theater of the Mind* was meant to be like a movie, Ludacris said. He said the guest artists were more like "co-stars." The album had lots of co-stars, too. Jay-Z, Common, T-Pain, Lil Wayne, Jamie Foxx, Rick Ross, and more all had parts on the album.

Unlike Ludacris's other albums, *Theater of the Mind* didn't really have any big singles. When it came out, lots of people liked the album. It didn't sell as well as Ludacris's other albums, though.

His last four albums had been number one in their first week. *Theater of the Mind* came in at number five. That seemed like a big difference.

Theater of the Mind didn't do as well as Ludacris wanted But he still wants to do another album like it. He likes the idea of doing another album based on the idea of a movie.

Despite his success or perhaps because of it Ludacris is one of hip-hop's most controversial stars. And it's not just his lyrics people complain about. His performances and clothes have also been criticized. Ludacris insists, however, there is a message behind his choices.

Battle of the Sexes

Ludacris's next album came out on March 9, 2010. This one was called *Battle of the Sexes*.

At first, Ludacris had different plans for *Battle of the Sexes*. He wanted the album to have a mix of his own songs and songs from the rapper Shawnna.

Shawnna was on the Disturbing tha Peace label. She'd also worked with Ludacris in the past. But things didn't work out. Shawnna left DTP in 2009. She moved to T-Pain's record label, Nappy Boy Entertainment.

Without Shawnna, *Battle of the Sexes* was all Ludacris. This wasn't what he wanted. So Ludacris brought on female MCs like Lil Kim and Nicki Minaj.

The album came out in March 2010. Right away, it went to number one. It sold 137,000 copies in one week. *Battle of the Sexes* was Ludacris's fourth number-one album.

The first single from *Battle of the Sexes* was "How Low." The song was a hit, going to number six on the **singles charts**. "My Chick Bad" followed "How Low." On the original, Nicki Minaj raps a verse. There is also a **remix**. In the remix, Eve, Nicki Minaj, Diamond, and Trina trade verses.

Battle of the Sexes was a big success. It proved that Ludacris was still making music people wanted to hear. It proved he was still on top.

Still on Top

Almost ten years after *Back for the First Time*, Ludacris is still one of rap's biggest stars. His music is still popular. He can still be heard on the radio. You can still see Ludacris's music videos on TV.

In October 2010, MTV named Ludacris one of the top-ten MCs in the rap game. And 2010 was a big year for Ludacris. *Battle of the Sexes* was a hit. He had three hit songs from the album, too.

Ludacris doesn't pull any punches in his music. Though his lyrics can cause big-name corporations to back away from his potential as a spokesperson, his millions of fans find his Dirty South hip-hop music something to which they can relate.

That year, he also did many guest verses on popular songs. He rapped a verse on Justin Bieber's hit single "Baby." The song was a huge hit in the summer of 2010. Ludacris's part in the song added just the kind of edge Justin Bieber wanted. Ludacris also put verses out on songs by Taio Cruz and DJ Khaled.

Guest verses kept Ludacris's name on people's minds. It also showed that other artists wanted to work with Ludacris. Many artists think that having Ludacris appear on their album can help them have the same kind of success he's had. And they might be right. Ludacris has been a guest on lots of big hits.

Ludacris plans to keep making music. In 2010, he told fans he'd be calling his next album *Ludaversal*. The next year, Luda said the album would be out in 2012. Fans were excited to hear that new music from Ludacris was on its way!

Ludacris was still working on more than music, too. He was still acting in films and television. In 2011, Ludacris acted in *Fast Five*, another movie in the *Fast and Furious* series and a movie called *New Year's Eve*. Ludacris' music has been popular for years. Today, he's known as a star with more than one talent. He can act, run businesses, and make great music. Not many people get to do all three in their lifetime!

Hip-Hop lingo

If you **inspire** people, you make them want to do something and make them feel good about themselves.

Poverty is when people are poor and cannot take proper care of themselves.

Positive means focusing on good things and believing that they can happen.

Chapter 5

The Greater Good

For many celebrities, having success isn't any good without using it to help others. Ludacris knows how important it is to give back. He's been working on giving back for years.

Ludacris has said that he wants to change music. He's also talked about how much he wants to help young people. Today's kids are going to be tomorrow's leaders. Ludacris wants to support young people in going after their goals.

The Ludacris Foundation

In 2001, Ludacris started the Ludacris Foundation (TLF). The Foundation's goal is to "**inspire** youth to live their dreams." The Foundation wants to help young people help themselves.

The Ludacris Foundation has three main programs. The first is called Leadership and Education. The program teaches kids that setting goals is the first step to success. Then, kids can take action. They can work on achieving their goals. The program also connects young people with successful leaders in art and business. These leaders help inspire kids to succeed.

TLF's Living Healthy Lifestyles program helps kids learn about health. They learn to eat healthier foods. They also learn that exercise is very important. Kids in this program even learn to cook healthy meals.

The LudaCares program focuses on poor families. The program makes sure kids who don't have much money get what they need for school. This might mean school supplies. Or it might mean learning how to study better.

LudaCares also gives toys, food, and clothing to families. TLF knows how hard the holidays can be. Ludacris remembers not having a lot when he was growing up. That's why he wants to help others have happy holiday seasons.

The Ludacris Foundation is all about helping young people meet their goals. Like Ludacris, TLF believes in young people making their own lives better. TLF is just one of the ways Ludacris gives back.

The Hip-Hop Summit Action Network

Ludacris also helps the Hip-Hop Summit Action Network by speaking to young people.

Russell Simmons started the Hip-Hop Summit Action Network (HSAN) in 2001. Simmons was a part of the rap group Run-DMC. They were one of the first rap groups to become popular. Today, Simmons works for HSAN. HSAN has worked on many different problems that young people face. It works to give all kids a chance at a good school. The group also helps to get young people to vote. HSAN helps kids to stay in school. It also works to help fight **poverty**.

Ludacris and HSAN agree that hip-hop can teach people. Hip-hop can be used to help make life better. Using hip-hop to speak to young people is important to Ludacris. His work with HSAN is one way of helping kids be **positive** about life.

Looking to the Future

Chris "Ludacris" Bridges has come a long way from rapping in the lunchroom at school. He's helped bring rap to people who had never heard it. He's sold millions of albums. His acting has given him even more fans and respect. Ludacris has used his success to help others through the Ludacris Foundation, as well.

Ludacris tries to do his best in everything he takes on. Whether he's making music, acting, or running his business, Ludacris wants to make a difference.

Today, the boy who rapped for his classmates is a star. The man who sold CDs from his car is the rapper he wanted to be. He's not done yet, though. Ludacris has more music to make. He has more acting to do, too.

No matter what he does next, Ludacris's fans will be waiting. And he'll be ready to give them what they want.

1970s   Hip-hop is born in the Bronx, New York.

1977   Christopher Bridges is born in Champaign, Illinois, on September 11.

1989   Joins his first hip-hop group, the Loudmouth Hooligans.

1990s   The hip-hop style known as Dirty South develops.

1999   Self-produces his first album, *Incognegro*.

2000   Signs with Def Jam Records.

2001   Acts in his first film, *The Wash*; establishes the Ludacris Foundation; the Hip-Hop Summit Action Network is formed.

2002   Ludacris receives his first Grammy nomination.

2004   The Ludacris Foundation is honored for its work. Wins awards from BET, Prism, and MTV.

2005   Creates controversy by wearing a Confederate flag while performing at the VIBE Awards; is ranked 60th in Bernard Goldberg's *100 People Who Are Screwing Up America*; the NBA Wives Association honors Ludacris's mother, Roberta Shields, for her work with the Ludacris Foundation and her role in her son's life; receives critical acclaim and a Screen Actor's Guild award for his performance in *Crash*, as well as accolades for his role in *Hustle and Flow*; wins his first Grammy Award.

2006   Signs a deal to host his own show on XM Satellite Radio, and becomes the first hip-hop artist to ring the New York Stock Exchange's opening bell.

2007   Ludacris loses his father to cancer.

2008 Ludacris collaborates with Ciara on her new single, "High Price."

2009 Working with the Norwegian cognac house Birkedal Hartmann, Ludacris helps create Conjure Cognac.

2010 Ludacris releases his seventh studio album, *Battle of the Sexes*.

In Books

Baker, Soren. *The History of Rap and Hip Hop*. San Diego, Calif.: Lucent, 2006.

Comissiong, Solomon W. F. *How Jamal Discovered Hip-Hop Culture*. New York: Xlibris, 2008.

Cornish, Melanie. *The History of Hip Hop*. New York: Crabtree, 2009.

Czekaj, Jef. *Hip and Hop, Don't Stop!* New York: Hyperion, 2010.

Haskins, Jim. *One Nation Under a Groove: Rap Music and Its Roots*. New York: Jump at the Sun, 2000.

Hatch, Thomas. *A History of Hip-Hop: The Roots of Rap*. Portsmouth, N.H.: Red Bricklearning, 2005.

Websites

Def Jam: Ludacris
www.islanddefjam.com/artist/home.aspx?artistID=7310

Disturbing the Peace
dtprecords.com

Ludacris on MTV
www.mtv.com/music/artist/ludacris/artist.jhtml

Ludacris on VH1
www.vh1.com/artists/az/ludacris/artist.jhtml

Ludacris World
www.ludacrisworld.com

Discography
Albums

1999	Incognegro
2000	Back for the First Time
2001	Word of Mouf
2003	Chicken N Beer
2004	The Red Light District
2006	Release Therapy
2008	Theater of the Mind
2010	Battle of the Sexes

Index

Index

About the Author

C.F. Earl is a writer living and working in Binghamton, New York. Earl writes mostly on social and historical topics, including health, the military, and finances. An avid student of the world around him, and particularly fascinated with almost any current issue, C.F. Earl hopes to continue to write for books, websites, and other publications for as long as he is able.

Picture Credits

CE006/Ace Pictures: p. 17
Dreamstime.com, Featureflash: p. 1
INFGoff/infusla-20: p. 26
Jason Nelson/AdMedia/Sipa Press: p. 36
KRT/Lionel Hahn: p. 34
KRT/NMI: p. 19
Lions Gate Films Inc./NMI: p. 25
MTV Films/NMI: p. 27
NMI/Def Jam Records: p. 14
NMI/Michelle Feng: pp. 21, 22
Photofest: p. 11
PRNewsFoto/NMI: p. 30
Shannon McCollum/WENN: p. 38
UPI Photo/Francis Specker: p. 29
UPI Photo/John Hayes: p. 6
WENN: p. 9
Zuma Press/NMI: p. 32

To the best knowledge of the publisher, all other images are in the public domain. If any image has been inadvertently uncredited, please notify Harding House Publishing Services, Vestal, New York 13850, so that rectification can be made for future printings.